Alfred George Compton

Some Common Errors of Speech

Suggestions for the avoiding of certain classes of errors, together with

examples of bad and of good usage

Alfred George Compton

Some Common Errors of Speech
Suggestions for the avoiding of certain classes of errors, together with examples of bad and of good usage

ISBN/EAN: 9783337403256

Printed in Europe, USA, Canada, Australia, Japan

Cover: Foto ©Andreas Hilbeck / pixelio.de

More available books at **www.hansebooks.com**

SOME COMMON ERRORS OF SPEECH

SUGGESTIONS FOR THE AVOIDING OF CERTAIN CLASSES OF ERRORS, TOGETHER WITH EXAMPLES OF BAD AND OF GOOD USAGE

BY

ALFRED G. COMPTON

G. P. PUTNAM'S SONS
NEW YORK AND LONDON
The Knickerbocker Press
1898

The Knickerbocker Press, New York

PREFACE.

THE following pages were first contributed to *The College Mercury* (a paper published by the students of the College of the City of New York), in the hope that they might help to improve the English to which I was obliged to listen daily in the class-room. I had thought, at first, to pick out a baker's dozen of the most noteworthy of the infelicities of speech and to parade these before my boys for deliberate inspection, somewhat as the Police Department shows up pickpockets. The limit of my baker's dozen was, however, soon passed; so too was the other limit I had set for myself, and I now offer my not very goodly company of offenders for the inspection of a larger assemblage than that for which I had at first intended them. If the spectacle of their ugliness shall have the effect of helping a few of my readers to turn away from them, and to seek, even at the expense of much labor and trouble, more pleasing forms of expression, I shall be content.

Both the bad forms and the corresponding good ones have been illustrated, when this was practicable, by examples. For obvious reasons, I have generally, in the former instances, withheld the names of the authors, but I am able, if required, to present evidence that the passages in question are actually "in print," and have been offered in good faith. They are taken, in part from standard literature, and in part from the newspapers and magazines of the day. That the daily papers should yield the most abundant examples of faulty diction is not surprising, when we consider the pressure under which the work of their writers and editors is done; what has surprised me more is the generally good character of our " newspaper English." The forms of expression to which this term of disparagement may be fairly applied are few, and there is an evident endeavor, on the part of most papers, to exclude them,—an endeavor which fails at times by reason of the desire for strong effect, and oftener, perhaps, through the impossibility of eternal vigilance.

I have in my collection made no attempt at system beyond that of classifying the rather miscellaneous faults under a few obvious heads, and I have undertaken, as a rule, to present only errors concerning which there is not much controversy. Writing simply with the view of submitting a few suggestions that may prove of service to writers who would like to do better than they are now doing, I have not attempted to enter into the discussions of philologists, for which, indeed, I cannot pretend to be qualified. I understand also that our English language is a live and growing speech, and that it ought not to be and in fact cannot be restrained by the bands of a past age or of an old-time literature, but must from time to time make for itself new expressions for new thoughts; I feel, however, that the conservative no less than the reformer has his mission in language, as in politics, and that a new word or phrase, like a rebel people, should be fought down until it has fought its way up and has proved its right to exist.

A. G. C.

CONTENTS

" In the first place, let me observe that our language is the most precious possession we have. It is a commonplace to say that the greatest gift God has bestowed on man is his power of communicating his thoughts to his fellows by speech, and not only of communicating thought, but the nicest shades of thought. . . . Now, to have and keep a language of this kind, somebody must take care of it, and must see that its peculiar excellences are preserved, that its words keep their meaning, that additions to it are not wantonly made, that all changes in it are justified and justifiable, and well considered. I speak with deliberation when I say that there is no civilized country in which, outside the colleges, so little of this is done as in ours." E. L. GODKIN, in *The Educational Review*, January, 1897.

SOME COMMON ERRORS OF SPEECH.

CHAPTER I.

IMPROPRIETIES.

THE use of a word in a sense not sanctioned by good usage is called an impropriety. The name is perhaps less used now than formerly, but the thing named is not less common. The following are a few faults of this kind that one frequently meets with. Some of them have been repeatedly noticed in books, but still survive, and perhaps are immortal.

1. *Liable* is improperly used as equivalent to *apt* or *likely*. "I am liable to forget unless I write it down." "He is **Liable.** liable to come in before three o'clock." "They are not liable to make such a mistake." In all these cases the proper

word is *apt* or *likely*,—*apt* when the thing spoken of is habitual, *likely* when a single occasion is referred to. Thus, in the first example, the meaning may be " I usually forget unless I write the thing down," and then *apt* is the proper word; or it may only be meant that on this occasion " I shall probably forget," and then *likely* is the word. The same distinction would hold in the case of the second example: " He is apt to come in," means he will probably come in because it is his habit to do so. " He is likely to come in," means it is probable for reasons existing in this particular instance; and in the third example exactly the same distinction would hold. *Liable* is wrong in all these cases: it means *exposed to*, *subject to*, or *in danger of*. It is not said of desirable things, but only of misfortunes. One is liable to defeat, sickness, infection, accident, loss of position, disappointment, failure, but not to promotion, success, recovery, praise, or other good things.

This word, moreover, is preferably used with a noun rather than with a verb. " Liable to error " is better than " liable to err," though Milton does use the latter.

Liable is correctly used in the first of the following examples, and incorrectly in the others.

" It inevitably arouses in us the notion of an illusiveness like that to which our visual perceptions are so liable." HERBERT SPENCER, *First Principles*, Ch. v.

" He is forgetful about details, and is liable to change his mind on important public questions every few days."

" A trip on the overland through New Mexico in those days—it was 1877—was apt to prove a little trying to a man of quiet tastes, for the Apaches always were liable to be lying in wait for the stage, and road agents were unusually industrious that year."

" I am pretty well acquainted with my Assembly district, which I have canvassed three times for Congress. It is liable to give Mr. Low from 2,000 to 2,500 votes, two-thirds of which will be Democratic."

" It is proper for the chiefs of the Citizens' Union to take precautions to keep its functions uncontaminated, and to be prepared for that enthusiastic surging of 'labor men' which its unpretentious and popular character is liable to bring upon it."

2. Somewhat analogous to the misuse of *liable* is that of *due*. This word is correctly

Due. used as an adjective, in the sense of "owing," as: "The success of the enterprise was entirely due to the persevering efforts of this one man." *Due to* is here the exact equivalent of *owing to*. It is no better than the latter, and Webster says it is not much used. It is, however, strictly correct; but when used, as it is occasionally, as an adverb, it is without good authority. "He was unable to arrive in time, due to the delaying of his train by a displaced rail," is inexcusable. "Owing to a displaced rail he was unable . . .," would be correct. *Owing to* is used both as adverb and as adjective, *due to* only as adjective.

"The club is in a bad way financially, due to differences about Cleveland."

The word must be understood here as adverbial, and the proper statement would be, " Owing to differences about Cleveland, the club is in a bad way."

" The resistance of the column of powder . . . was often enormously great, due to the imperfect contact between adjacent particles."

" It is perhaps due to this promise that Sir Alfred heartily concurs in the desire."

" While these tests have never been completed, due to more urgent work."

" . . . the air at the centre became denser, due to reduction of velocity."

The Weather Bureau is right in the following passage:

" In the central valleys and Southern States the week has not been favorable, *owing to* general absence of rain and prevalence of high temperature."

As to the following one feels less sure; it would be better if the adjective *due* were nearer to its noun, *modifications :*

" There are abundant instances to prove that considerable modifications may suddenly develop themselves, due to external conditions or to obscure internal causes." MIVART, *Natural Selection.*

3. The use of *apt* as the equivalent of *likely*
is an impropriety.   To be apt to do a thing

Apt.
means to do it frequently, though
not quite habitually: there is still
some uncertainty.   Frequency, however, is a
necessary element in the meaning of the word.
The following passage is wrong:

" But there is apt to be a spirited contest at the
Democratic caucus in the afternoon."

'' There will probably be a spirited contest ''
is the proper expression.

4.   Though these words have the same origin
they have acquired different meanings, and the

Definitely,
Definitively.
distinction between them is so useful that it ought to be preserved.
Definitely means specified as to contents, pre-
cisely limited, and is opposed to *vague* and
indefinite.   *Definitive* means settled, freed
from doubt, and is opposed to *tentative,*
temporary, or *provisional.*   A definite agreement is made if the terms of the agreement
are precise; a definitive agreement has been

made if the transaction has been actually agreed on, even though the terms are not exactly settled. The parties to a dispute as to a boundary may have definitively agreed to effect a settlement in a certain way, or within a certain time, though the boundary may not have been definitely marked out. On the other hand, a definite boundary may have been decided on, though the conditions on which both parties will accept it may not have been definitively agreed on. The use of definite and definitely instead of definitive and definitively is very common : the opposite error is much less likely to occur.

The following are examples of the wrong use of the words :

"Natal was practically a No Man's Land until 1843, when England definitely took charge of the country."

"Boulton then definitely decided not to continue his own experiments."

". . . and there will be no improvement until the plan is definitely adopted by some organization and earnest work done."

The words are rightly used in the following:

"She [Greece] has extricated it [the Eastern question] from the meshes of diplomacy and has placed it on the order of the day for a definitive solution." W. E. GLADSTONE, Letter to the Duke of Westminster.

"The course of Great Britain in the matter has not yet been decided upon, but Ambassador Hay will probably receive a definite statement on the subject this week."

5. *To claim* is wrongly used in place of *to maintain, to state an opinion.* The word means

To claim. *to demand as a right.* When the expression of an opinion is intended, the proper verb is *to maintain,* or *to declare,* or, if the opinion is held in the face of opposition, *to contend.* I have heard a student of astronomy say, "Some astronomers claim that Mars is inhabited." Doubtless there are enterprising commercial peoples who would "claim" Mars as within their sphere of influence, if they knew it to be inhabited, but they would be very foolish to make any claim as to its being inhabited: they can only *think* or *believe* or *maintain* that it is so. Daniel Webster long ago called attention to this misuse of the word *claim* as being, in his day, prevalent in Connecticut:

"This word *claim* means everything in the law language of Connecticut. Here a man claims that he has lost a deed."

The "Ohio Claim" with which the last presidential election made us acquainted, though not admirable politically or morally, is better linguistically than this Connecticut claim. A demand for all the offices "in sight" may be correctly characterized as a claim.

"They claimed he used the United States mails for the purpose of swindling."

"Mr. Stevens of Belgium claimed that the prisoner owed his service to the state."

Carlyle writes:

"It is maintained by Helvetius and his set that an infant of genius is quite the same as any other infant." *Sartor Resartus*, Bk. II., Ch. ii.

There is no *claim* in this.

6. This is a favorite word with many persons, to express anything large, unusual, surprising,—a meaning that does not belong to the word.

Phenomenal.

Phenomenon and phenomenal are terms of philosophy, opposed to noumenon and noumenal, and they refer to the appearance of things, as opposed to the things themselves,—the former being knowable and capable of being described, while the latter, if there are any latter, are perhaps forever unknowable. In common language these opposed terms are rarely used, the ideas corresponding to them having rarely need of expression, and the words have still the appearance of words foreign to the language. A sunrise, a snow-storm, the opening of a flower, the growth of a child, is properly spoken of as an impressive or beautiful phenomenon. It was so much more natural, however, to call it a beautiful spectacle, scene, event, or change, that there was little use in ordinary speech for *phenomenon* in its proper meaning, and still less for *phenomenal*, and so the words have been captured by the press-gang of writers, and forced into a service that is alien to them.

" Mr. Lamson . . . has every reason to hope that before long he will attain with his invention phenomenal results in aërial navigation."

In the following passage the word is correctly used:

"When, therefore, Philosophy proves that our knowledge of the external world can be but phe-nomenal—when it concludes that the things of which we are conscious, are appearances, it inevitably arouses in us the notion of an illusiveness like that to which our visual perceptions are so liable in comparison with our tactual perceptions." SPENCER, *First Principles*, Ch. v.

The few examples of improprieties here presented will perhaps be enough to induce the young writer to give some thought to the choice of words, and this is all that can be expected. As soon as he feels the desire to use words rightly, he will learn how to find, in

dictionaries and books on synonymy, the guid-
ance that he needs. Only the careless feeling that the first word which comes to hand is
good enough, prevents the writer from seeking
the word that shall be the very best for his
purpose.

CHAPTER II.

METAPHORS.

1. At every stage in the growth of a language and of its literature there are certain **Worn-out metaphors.** metaphors which are current and are understood, but which have survived whatever usefulness they may have had. They were perhaps picturesque once : they presented a thought in a striking way, or fixed the mind very strongly on one particular aspect of a subject; but by dint of reiteration they have become wearisome. They have ceased to add force to a presentation; and the moment they fail to add clearness or force they become mere encumbrances, not only useless, but harmful. It would be easy to make a long list of them. A few of them are: iron horse, iron heel of tyranny, leaden hail, procrustean bed, ship of state, upas tree, saturnalia, holocaust,

phœnix, perhaps also alma mater. Some of these are seldom met with now, perhaps never, though they once moved in very respectable company. Others obtrude themselves on us daily in the newspapers and magazines, and not a few find their way into college orations, sermons, and political platforms.

2. Besides the metaphors that are worn out, there are others that never were good. They **Bad metaphors.** are based on a false analogy. They assume a resemblance between the thing represented and the thing representing it that does not exist; or they are based on a resemblance in some aspect or quality which is only an accident and not an essential.

3. *Tidal-wave*, as a name for a swift and powerful movement of opinion or feeling, is **Tidal-wave.** such a metaphor. If an election turns out the party in power, a tidal-wave is said to have swept the country. The context always shows that the writer is thinking of the tidal-wave as something swift

and terrible. It is in fact no such thing, however, but only a very gentle rise and fall of the
water of the ocean, through a height of half a
dozen feet in twelve hours. It is indeed not
perceived as a " wave " at all, except by the
eye of science. The fact seems to be that the
name tidal-wave was given, in mere ignorance,
to one of those rare and formidable disturb-
ances of the ocean that are caused by earth-
quake shocks or volcanic eruptions, such as
the memorable wave that followed the fall of a
large part of the volcano Krakatoa into the
sea, and that, as the name sounded mysterious
and imposing, it continued to be used, to give
dignity to comparatively trifling events. It
throws no light, however, on the phenomenon
to which, as a supposed metaphor, it is applied, and when we look for the real meaning
of it we find it misleading. A literal expression, as " a great movement of popular
thought," " a powerful uprising of the con-
science of the people," would carry with it no

false implication, and its meaning would be clear.

4. Akin to the last error is the use of *cyclone* in nearly the same sense. A cyclone,

Cyclone. like a tidal-wave, is one of the large and deliberate movements of nature which have very little of terror or destructiveness in them. A cyclone is an atmospheric movment of large extent, often a thousand miles or more in diameter, and throughout nearly the whole of the area that it covers, gentle and beneficent. Cyclones and anti-cyclones are passing over our heads continually, and, except when we happen to be very near their centres, we never think of them as terrible, and hardly know of their existence, save as windy or rainy weather. The thing that the fine writer had in his mind when he called a sudden and violent outburst of national frenzy a " cyclone of patriotic fervor " was not a cyclone: it was a hurricane or tornado; but there was something high-sounding and mysterious in the word, and so it seemed to him good.

5. *Carnival* is another word that is misused in the some way. When the orthodox

Carnival. Catholic Italians are about entering on their long lenten fast, they allow themselves one period of unrestrained fun before they bid good-bye to the pleasures of the table. But, because they pelt each other with candies and little bags of flour, and take such liberties with each other as at other times they would not venture to take, the metaphor-dealer thinks two or three house-burnings ought to be called a carnival of fire, and half a dozen murders a carnival of blood. That his metaphor, instead of making clear his meaning, only beclouds it, concerns him little: it sounds well, he thinks. His last misuse of the word surpasses all previous ones: in a public advertisement which stares at us from the fences, he calls a great sale at a " department store," a " mammoth bargain carnival."

6. *Handicap.*   To handicap a competitor in a race is to give others an advantage over him by **Handicap.** letting them start in advance of him, or by making him carry a load.   The essential idea in the word is that there is a contest, and that the chances of the contestants are to be made nearly equal.   A person is not " handicapped " in an undertaking when he encounters obstacles, or when he is not properly equipped for his work, unless he is in competition with others, nor even then, if only his own infirmity or bad luck is in the way.   The word, therefore, is wrongly used in the following examples :

" For a long time the scientific bureaus of the government have felt themselves badly handicapped by the need of resorting to special examinations."

The bureaus may have been annoyed, or hampered, or put to much trouble; but they were not handicapped.

" The new cabinet officers find themselves very

seriously handicapped in their plans for reorganiz-
ing their departments by the Civil Service law."

Orgy. 7. " There will be an orgy of increased armaments."

Case-hardened. 8. " The sin, as it seems to me, would be to feel or fancy ourselves case-hard-ened against the will of our Maker."

9. " Wall Street had a lesson in this direction which will never be forgotten, during the brewing of the disturbance which ended in the Franco-Prussian war."

Brewing.

10. How bad a figure is the word *thorn* in the following example, is evident at a glance :

Thorn.

" Katarina, which, it is said, will be bombarded, is the port of Elassona, and, if it falls into the hands of the Greeks, will be a thorn in Edhem Pasha's communications."

A word is, of course, not to be rejected be-cause it is figurative. It is a commonplace that most of the every-day words that have no figurative association now were originally fig-ures of speech; that *lady, husband, king, con-gress, parlor, person,* and a thousand others meant originally something very different from what they mean now, and that the first use of any of them in its present meaning was a bold and effective metaphor. It is in this way that language has grown, and, to a less extent, still grows. A metaphoric term, however, if it is going to establish itself as a mere name for something, a new word without its first poetical associations, soon asserts its right to its new rank; and if it fails to do this soon it has to retire: it is neither a common word nor a metaphor, and it is in the way. Iron road has established itself as the every-day name of the railway in France, Germany, Italy, and Spain; but iron horse has been rejected in all these as well as in England and America, and nobody wants it now, even as a figure of speech. So it is with the other words cited. And it is not the critics only who reject such tattered figures: the common people are just as quick, and the speaker or writer who indulges too much in " fine writing " will often find them smiling at his flights.

As to the question of using or not using a figure of speech that offers itself (it should never be sought for), the best course perhaps is to let it stand, in one's first draught, and consider carefully, on revision, whether it shall be rejected. That which can bear the sober second thought—or the soberer third thought—may generally be allowed to pass.

CHAPTER III.

GRAMMAR.

FAULTS in grammar range all the way from the gravest, such as no one who has learned the rudiments of grammar would be guilty of, to those evanescent ones that lie in the neutral zone between what is certainly forbidden and what is certainly allowed, from the jargon of the newsboy to the doubtful solecisms of the editor, from " I aint got none," and " them 's mine," to " wishing to thus despoil the park."

Faults of the first class I had at first intended not to discuss; but, besides that it is difficult to say where the boundary of this class lies, there are many faults that might be considered as falling within this line, which are yet so common that writers—particularly young writers—need to be cautioned against them. For this reason I shall include under the present heading a few expressions that some readers may think it unnecessary to touch upon.

Among the commonest errors in grammar are the errors in agreement. They occur in several ways:

1. A nominative is often treated as an accusative, through the accident of its standing

Accusative for nominative.

near a verb that governs the accusative: " The man whom I supposed was the ringleader turns out to be quite innocent." Those who fall into this very common but inexcusable error may think of *whom* as the object of *supposed* (if they can be said to think at all), and forget that *whom* cannot be the subject of *was*. If *was* is used, *who* must be its subject, and the sentence must read: ". . . who, I thought, was the ringleader." It must be admitted that this has a bad effect: the reader can hardly avoid the impression at first, that *who* is meant as the object of *thought*, and that the writer is guilty of a blunder. He is set right when he comes to the word *was*, and sees that *who* is really not an object but a subject; but the mischief has been done,—the transparency of the sentence has been clouded. It is not enough that the meaning of the sentence should become clear when the end is reached: there should not be any hesitation or doubt at any point in its progress. It is true that commas before and after *I thought* direct the attention to the proper construction; but it is much to be preferred that the meaning should appear clearly, independently of punctuation, and so the passage should read: " the man that I thought to be the ringleader."

The following are examples of this fault which the reader will easily correct:

" There is abundant evidence to show that he was at least one of the distinguished men whom Gruter says had access to Gilbert's writing in its unpublished form."

" But you must not shut your eyes to the fact that I am only a chemist, a shopkeeper, . . .

one whom your people would say was no fit friend for you."

" Epicurus writes a letter to Idomeneus . . . to recommend to him, who had made so many men rich, one Pythocles, a friend of his, whom he desired might be made a rich man too."

". . . an odd brother who sat on the same benches in the ancient chapel . . . and one whom, if we may credit what another philosopher high in favor in court said about him, was a testy and crusty old gentleman."

2. A careless writer sometimes refers a pronoun back, in his imagination, to a noun that has no existence in the sentence, **Pronoun without antecedent.** leaving it thus in the unfortunate predicament of a word that " stands for a noun," but which has no noun that it can stand for:

" There are three slave markets outside of Africa which make the business of the Arab slave-hunters profitable in certain parts of Africa, namely, Zanzibar, Arabia, and Egypt. In Egypt they are in demand as household slaves."

Here the writer evidently meant to say that

the slaves are in demand, but he does say, if he says anything, that the three slave markets are in demand: he has not provided the pronoun *they* with any antecedent.

" A camel's gait is a peculiar one, they go something like a pig with the fore and like a cow with the hind legs."

This also is a common error; but it is one that could be very easily avoided. It is only necessary that the writer should cultivate the habit of looking back whenever he uses a pronoun, to see whether there is an antecedent to which it unmistakably refers. In this way the habit of correct reference will soon be formed.

3. Often there are two nouns in the sentence, and the writer refers the pronoun, in his

Pronoun: wrong antecedent.
mind, to the wrong one. An advertisement of some fine silks reads as follows:

" Simpson, Crawford & Simpson having bought

the entire collection they will be on exhibition in our windows this week."

The purchasing of some silks hardly deserves, one would think, so severe a punishment as that which the gentlemen's advertising agent seems to propose. The fault here would have been detected if the writer had paused to inquire what *they* referred to. He would then probably have written : " The entire collection having been purchased . . . will be exhibited." It is not common to find examples of this fault so ludicrous as this and the following, from a standard text-book :

" To the group of Dinosaurs belongs the Iguanodon, of the Wealden beds, first made known by Dr. Mantell, whose body was 28 to 30 feet long."

A great railroad has for years kept the following request before the eyes of all its passengers :

" In case of accident, pull the handle of this valve up as far as it will go ; when the train has come to a stop pull it back to its former position."

It is not known that any passenger has tried to do the thing proposed, and so the notice has done no harm perhaps; but why should not the writer of it have looked to his pronoun, before sending it out into the world in such ambiguous company ?

4. This mental referring, by the writer, of a pronoun to the wrong antecedent, or of a verb to the wrong subject, causes, frequently, disagreement in number. This is a very common class-room error, but it is subtle enough also to entrap many a respectable writer, as the following examples show :

Disagreement in number.

" When I recollect to what complete perfection the culture of many of the best productions of the earth have been brought in France . . ."

" The idea of these dangers were interesting rather than unpleasant."

" . . . his [Lord Salisbury's] attitude toward the American contentions in Behring Sea are impossible to forecast."

" It was kept by a brother and sister, neither of whom was out of their teens."

" Every one of them pressed forward to do something for him, and seemed discouraged if they were not employed."

"And sometimes he stands up while everybody else is on their knees."

".   .   .   and assumed that, but for the fear of being burned, or for the hope of being rewarded, anybody would pass their lives in lying, stealing and murdering."

" It must always be remembered that a fungus, which may be perfectly harmless if cooked and eaten while fresh, would just as probably be deleterious if gathered and kept for a day or two without cooking.   Chemical changes take place so rapidly that they cannot be cooked too soon, and not even the common mushrooms should be kept longer than possible."

5. The participles give a great deal of trouble, which may, however, be avoided if the writer will take the pains to inquire, **Participle: wrong reference.** concerning every participle, what it relates to, and will see that he does not allow it to appear to relate to any other word.   The fault under consideration presents itself in a great variety of ways, and requires

various treatment. The following specimens will sufficiently illustrate it:

" But this officer, hoping that by refusing this humane request the Cubans would desist in the bombardment, absolutely prohibited the exit of non-combatants from the town."

" By refusing " was obviously meant to refer to " this officer," but, if the writer had asked himself the question, What does it refer to ? he would have seen, or ought to have seen, that it refers to " the Cubans." The false reference would have been corrected if he had written, " hoping that, if he refused the request, the Cubans would stop the bombardment . . ."

" Rising with the sun, a dish of kumis or mare's milk, and a small cup of black coffee are the only refreshments formally partaken of."

If the writer of this had inquired what " rising with the sun " referred to, he would have found that it referred to " a dish of kumis," though he meant it, no doubt, to refer to some person, whom, however, he has neglected to mention.

"Being a great seaport, one sees plenty of sea-faring faces, . . . and being at the same time an important naval and military station for Great Britain, another picturesque element is made up of the gay uniforms of soldiers and sailors."

"Dressed all in black broadcloth, with a wide-leafed black felt hat, hands in pockets, I had first met him striding leisurely down the wide main street of Fort Atkinson."

√ 6. The English language allows a degree of freedom in the use of the passive form that is

Passive voice. often conducive to rapidity and force, but which is, in the present day, much abused. The following sentences can hardly be considered good:

"What then is the use of these investigations, by which the correlation and equivalence of force is sought to be established?"

"The next I knew the bill was agreed to be favorably reported."

"A portion of Duncan's coat of mail is pretended to be shown there."

"Mr. Peckham conceded that the contract was only an agreement by which . . . the secret undercutting of rates is sought to be avoided."

"The taxing power was never before threatened to be so ruthlessly and defiantly used."

" The clover, which was to be begun cutting on the morrow . . ."

Bad as these appear, however, it would be easy to make a collection of expressions leading up to these, by easy steps, from others with which no fault could be found:

" The spy was executed the next morning."
" The debts were paid."
" It was expected that the debts would be paid."
" He was ordered to be executed."
" The debts were expected to be paid."

The first three of these sentences are beyond criticism; the fourth is to be justified, if at all, either because, in spite of opposition, it has established its right to exist, or because " to order to be executed " may be regarded as a compound verb, capable of being used in the passive voice; but for the last neither of these excuses can be urged, and as it is unnecessary, it should be avoided. One can say with greater simplicity, " It was expected that the debts would be paid," and some analogous turn of expression can always be found in such cases.

7. Perhaps the worst cases of the kind under consideration are those in which the verb that is put into the passive form

Passive, verbs of giving. is one that governs both a dative and an accusative, as *give, promise, award, allow, guarantee,* and some others. A noun in the accusative may be put into the nominative if the construction of the sentence is changed from active to passive: " He fought a battle" may become: " A battle was fought." " They gave a great banquet " may become: " A great banquet was given "; and such change is sometimes advantageous, as fixing the attention on the act rather than the actor. A noun or pronoun in the dative, however, representing the person to whom something is given, cannot properly be thus made nominative. " They gave him a consulship as a reward for his services to his party " is good English, if bad morality, but " He was given a consulship as a reward " must be condemned under both heads; and it has not even the defence of directness or force, since " He was rewarded with a consulship," or "A consulship was his reward," would be at least equally direct. Indolence is the only excuse for such expressions. Every one of the following examples can easily be made correct without suffering in force:

"There have been many editions of the *Diary* [Pepys's], but it is only now that the public is given a complete one."

" But no complete one has been given till now " is better, not only for the reason already given, but because *edition* and not *public* should lead, in the latter part of the sentence as in the former part.

"Among the men who attended were a delegation from the City Club Committee on Legislation which was given power to act on charter matters."

" Which had been empowered " would correct the bad passive form and the wrong tense at the same time.

" At the same time it is essential to the establishment of the merit system that the subordinate shall in some way be assured protection from the danger of removal without cause."

The awkward locution could have been avoided by so simple a change as the insertion of the preposition *of* after assured.

" It is understood however, that Sir Herbert Kitchener will be given the command of the army of occupation."

So simple a change as " Sir Herbert Kitchener will receive the command . . .", or " The command will be given to Sir Herbert . . .", would make the sentence correct without making it less idiomatic or forcible.

" ' The resolution must follow the usual course,' sharply replied the Speaker, and so the House was not given an opportunity of deciding whether it wanted to sympathize with the Greeks or not."

" The pretension of a protectorate is directly contrary to the history and traditions of this country, and was given diplomatic life only through the extraordinary combination of qualities which made Mr. Blaine a successful demagogue."

The idiomatic character of the expression is one of the defences most commonly set up in such cases as these, and examples are often cited from good writers. It is true that many forms of expression which do not conform strictly to rules of grammar have found acceptance, and have become idioms of one language or another. It is also true, however, that idioms which do not conduce to force and clearness, but rather to weakness and obscurity, acquire no particular sacredness merely because of their being idioms. And as for good writers and their usage, there is no infallible writer, and no expression can be justified merely by the fact that it was used by Addison, or Swift, or Johnson, or even by De Quincey, or Lamb, or Eliot. Even in spite of the usage of many good writers, we are justified in avoiding a given form if it is bad on theoretical grounds, provided the required meaning can be equally well expressed by another form, not open to the same objections.

8. This construction, which is not often met with in America, is rather common among

Pluperfect for past future. English writers: " I expected him to have come to see me " should be " I expected him to come to see me." The action of *coming* was, at the time of the *expecting*, not past, but future.

So: " Might have been expected to have gone," which is quoted from Froude by Richard Grant White, should be " Might have been expected to go." The corrections in the following examples are obvious:

"It would have behooved him as a physician . . . to have regarded his own pursuits in a peculiarly philosophical spirit."

"She would have given much, however, to have escaped this business."

"What the English ought to have done was to have supported their natural ally, the Sultan."

" A vivacious old man whom I took to have been the devil, drew near and questioned me about our journey."

"It would have gone to your heart to have heard the moans the dumb creature made on the day of my master's death."

Here is Macaulay's treatment of such a case:

"It would therefore have been mere insanity to leave him in possession of that plenitude of military authority which his ancestors had enjoyed." *History of England*, Ch. i.

9. This fault is very common in New York among young people, and particularly among
Preterit for perfect. those who have been brought up in German surroundings. I frequently hear, and sometimes read: "I did not get excused yet," "I did not study so far to-day." The rule is inflexible in English, that a past action in a time not yet finished, no matter how long the time named may be, whether it be this day, this week, or this century, must be in the perfect tense, while an action in a time which is finished, however short the time may be, though it be only "five minutes ago," or "this morning," provided I am speaking this afternoon, must be in the preterit. "Nothing like it has been seen this century," "I have seen it within five minutes, though

I cannot remember where," "I met him more than five minutes ago,"—these are all correct. "I have not seen him this morning" and "I did.not see him this morning" are also both correct, provided the first is said while the morning is yet unfinished, and the second after the morning is finished. This distinction does not hold in some other languages, but it is rigorous in English. It is even impossible to give examples of the neglect of it from fairly good writers, and it is in this respect unlike most of the other faults cited in this work.

10. The substitution of the preterit for the pluperfect, as in the following, is a less common error, though I meet with it Preterit for occasionally among speakers or Pluperfect. writers of German descent:

"Her Sylvander was seventeen years in the grave when her husband died."

11. There has been much controversy as to the propriety of separating the particle *to* from

the verb of which it is a part, for the purpose of putting an adverb or an adverbial phrase between. Shall we write, as one of our daily papers does, " It would be a shame, some said, to thus despoil this beautiful park," or rather, as Washington Irving did, " Oliver Goldsmith will be found faithfully to inherit the virtues and the weaknesses of his race " ? The practice of good writers and particularly of careful ones is in favor of the latter, though a large collection can be made, and has been made by Fitzedward Hall, of passages supporting the former. Of such an array of citations this must be said : There is scarcely any form of expression, however bad, that cannot be shown to have been used by some moderately good writers or even by some great one. From Shakspere's " between you and I," all the way up, or down, to Byron's " there let him lay," examples can be found of almost every fault that can be named. The difficulties of rhythm and rhyme, the energy

Divided infinitive.

sometimes supposed to belong to vulgar forms of speech, the fierce rush of inspired utterance which will not pick and choose but must come forth at once,—all these and more are cited in justification of such lapses. They are at best excuses only; and while the writer may be pardoned for using such speech at first, rather than interrupt the swift current of his thought, he is inexcusable for not having amended it when the time for quiet correction came. Moreover, while much may be forgiven to the authors of *Othello* and *Childe Harold*, the rank and file of writers have no right to expect the immunity of genius for their blunders, but must seek to please by correct and graceful expression.

12. It is said, in answer to the objections to the divided infinitive, that the separating of the particle is not a violation of any **Divided infinitive: apology.** rule of grammar, and that it sometimes helps the writer over the difficulty, so often encountered, of getting the

adverb into close connection with the verb that it qualifies. As to the first statement, the answer is that *to*, as the sign of the infinitive, is not the preposition *to*, nor is it properly a word at all. It is only the sign of the mood, as *en*, *oir*, *ar*, etc., are in other languages. This is fully recognized in common speech and writing, and no one would think of saying " I hope to safely arrive," " He promised to as quickly as possible come," " I thought I should be able to before it was too late see him." In all these absurd instances the object that seems to be generally in view has been accomplished,—the adverb has been hedged in where there can be no possible doubt as to what it refers to, but at what a cost! Absurd as these examples are, they are only a little more objectionable than hundreds that one might jot down in a month's reading from college compositions, magazine articles, scientific reports, and even more pretentious writings:

"We cannot suppose that Columbia College would be so discourteous as to gratuitously ignore our challenge."

" Some air-castles he built so often that he seemed to fairly dwell in them."

" They were said to always buy everything of the best."

" The governor . . . [of the engine] is free to instantly respond to variations in the rate of motion."

" He hoped to really interest the readers of his journal in the affair."

" He then saw his way to completely supply this want."

It is not easy to see what advantage these expressions have over the following:

" Nor will it be less my duty faithfully to record disasters mingled with triumphs." MACAULAY, *Hist. of England*, Ch. i.

" Senator Sherman's acceptance of the State portfolio made it a necessity for him at once publicly to recant." *Evening Post*, Jan. 16, 1897.

" We may form a pretty accurate idea of the quality of these productions from the fact that Quintus Cicero, in order homœopathically to beguile the weariness of winter quarters in Gaul, composed four tragedies in sixteen days." MOMMSEN, *Rome*. Translated by Dickson, iv., 689.

"The Commission does not assume that it has been able to anticipate every contingency, nor . . . altogether to avoid omissions, repetitions, and mistakes." W. L. STRONG, *Report on New Charter*.

"Fully to enter into such a subject would occupy much space." WALLACE, *Natural Selection*, Preface.

"Suitably to provide against this is the mandate of duty." MCKINLEY, Inaugural Address.

"He will do well constantly to try himself in respect of these, steadily to widen his culture, severely to check in himself the provincial spirit." MATTHEW ARNOLD, *The Literary Influence of Academies*.

". . . and we may surely be led somewhat to distrust our judgment of them by observing what ignoble imaginations have sometimes . . . occupied the hearts of others." RUSKIN, *The Ethics of the Dust*, Ch. vii.

"As his inclinations were to philosophical study, this it was now his ambition uninterruptedly to pursue." BENJAMIN, *The Intellectual Rise in Electricity*.

"It brings us on to the platform where alone the best and highest intellectual work can be said fairly to begin." MATTHEW ARNOLD, *The Literary Influence of Academies*.

". . . we ought at all times humbly to acknowledge our sins before God." *Book of Common Prayer*.

"If so, the tendency would be to diminish slowly the planet's mean motion." KIRKWOOD, *Meteoric Astronomy*, Ch. iii.

"He must admit that it [government] had been employed in some instances wholly to remove, and in many considerably to correct the abusive practices and usages that had prevailed in the state." BURKE, *Reflections on the Revolution in France*.

"Congress shall make no law . . . abridging the right of the people peaceably to assemble, and to petition the Government for a redress of grievances." Constitution of the United States.

13. The use of the present participle as a **Participial noun without government.** noun requires that this noun be properly governed; but this requirement is often neglected.

"I must trust to the reader reposing some confidence in my accuracy."

"I must trust to the reader's reposing some confidence . . ." supplies the government required.

"And I presume that this change may be safely attributed to the domestic duck flying much less and walking more than its wild parent."

"No case is on record of a variable being ceasing to be variable under cultivation."

"Upon the fellow telling him he would warrant it [the axle] the knight . . . went in without further ceremony."

In these examples the possessive government, the right one, would have been easily secured, as it is secured in the following:

"No, Mr. Caudle, no, it's no use your telling me to go to sleep." JERROLD, *Mrs. Caudle's Curtain Lectures*, No. 3.

"If any one has such a scheme of policy to propose, I advise his proposing it anywhere rather than in England." GLADSTONE, Letter to the Duke of Westminster.

"The account given by Herodotus of Xerxes's cutting a canal through the isthmus of Athos . . . is much more strongly attested by Thucydides. . . ." WHATELY, *Rhetoric*, Part I., Ch. ii., Sec. 4.

The following are cases in which the fault could not have been so easily avoided; but it could have been avoided nevertheless:

"We need not be surprised at this system, when it does act under confinement, acting not quite regularly."

". . . at this system's acting not quite

regularly when it does act," would have corrected the error.

"Not only was thought made treason, but men
were forced to reveal their thoughts on pain of
their very silence being punished with the penalty
of treason."

This is a difficult case, because of the harsh
effect of putting " silence " into the possessive
case; but a different expression can easily be
found, not using the participle at all, as: ". . .
lest their very silence should be punished
. . ." Thus, as usual, it is only indolence
or haste that prevents the writer's finding the
proper expression, provided he has the ability
to judge what is proper.

14. This fault, of leaving a participial noun
without government, is very common, but we
Participle are not to suppose that it occurs
as adjective. every time we find a participle
unaccompanied by a possessive. In the following examples the participles are used as adjec-
tives, and need no possessive:

"That puts the President in the most attractive light before the machine workers, for what could be more winning than this picture of him laying his hand on the General's shoulder . . .?"

"We should have been face to face with an unparalleled political betrayal—nothing less than that of the chief of the party opposed to free silver at 16 to 1 doing his best to force free silver upon us at $15\frac{1}{2}$ to 1."

The following is a doubtful passage, susceptible, perhaps, of either interpretation:

"His discourse was broken off by his man telling him he had called a coach."

15. Of the prepositions that accompany verbs there are some that are parts of adverbial phrases, as " to learn by heart," " to discuss at length," " I shall come of course," and so on. There are others that may be regarded as parts of the verb, forming compounds analogous to those so freely used in German, as " That is something I should never think of," " That is more than I bargained for," " Such conduct is hard to conceive of." These two classes of expres-

Prepositions with verbs.

sion give no trouble: the preposition and the noun or verb are so constantly seen together that no other preposition ever intrudes.

There are verbs, however, that keep company, or have kept company, with more than one preposition, and which give occasion sometimes for doubt as to their proper mates. These are generally verbs of Latin origin, having already Latin prepositions of their own firmly united to them, and which hold rather loosely therefore to the second or English companions which have been forced upon them.

16. The tendency of the English language, as of other languages, in respect to such verbs

Differ from. as these, is in favor of that preposition which is a translation of the Latin one. Thus we say, *append to, annex to, detach from, exempt from, concur with, communicate with, deliver from,* and so on through a long list. Nevertheless, *differ with* is now sometimes met with, and though not conformable with the genius of the language, seems likely, if not to drive out the other expression, at least to divide its domain. The only cases, I think, in which *differ with* is used are those in which a difference of opinion is spoken of. When the difference is in character, religion, appearance, anything but opinion, no one, I think, would use anything but *differ from*. Even in this use, the form *differ with* is certainly not well established; it is seldom if ever used in speaking of third persons, but only when the speaker says " I differ with so-and-so "; and, as it is entirely unnecessary, it seems to me it should be avoided. The following is correct:

"I must differ from you there altogether." TROLLOPE, *Dr. Thorne*, Ch. xliv.

"SIR : A few years ago I felt the necessity of differing from you on the subject of foot-ball." Letter in *The Nation*, Dec. 23, 1897.

"Perhaps in minor particulars I might differ from him." *Report of the Electrical Conference at Philadelphia*, 1884, p. 162.

17. *Connect to* is much used now by some

writers on electricity, instead of *connect with.*

Connect with. It has no advantage over the latter, and has no support among good writers. There is no need for it, even as a technical term, and there is the strongest reason therefore why it should be avoided.

" This time includes placing the cartridge in the hole, connecting to the pump and . . ."
" Must each have the frame permanently connected to ground."
" If the sphere be an infinitely thin conductor and be connected to the ground . . ."

The same writer, however, says, correctly :

" The vessel is connected with an electrometer."
" The quadrants connected with *b* become positively charged, and the quadrants connected with *a* become negatively charged."

18. *Compare to* is no better than *connect to : with* is the proper preposition in both cases.

Compare to. Observe the effect of the substitution in the following examples :

" Yet two of these were good cross-examiners compared to the chairman."

"They still knew that the interest they took in their business was a trifling affair compared to their spontaneous, long-suffering affection for nautical sport."

19. An adjective requires the same preposition as the verb to which it is etymologically

Preposition with adjective. related. *Different to* is therefore as wrong as *differ with*, and the following examples must be condemned:

". . . and Russian officers must be very different to English ones."
" It is quite a different affair to that of Moffat's."

The correct usage is shown in Section 16.

The following are examples of the misuse of other prepositions. The errors will be readily detected:

"In walked Sir Hercules Robinson, dressed in a court uniform much ornamented by gold embroidery."
". . . the emperors of Austria and Russia sympathized in the autocratic tendencies of Abdul Hamid."
" Every particle of matter of which we have any knowledge attracts every other particle in conformity to the law of gravitation."

20. Some mistakes in the use of auxiliaries are rather common. First among these is the **Auxiliaries: Can.** use of *can* instead of *may*, a mistake common in childhood, and not altogether unknown in maturer years. "You can now go and take some exercise," "Can we have a week longer for our composition?" These, if rare, are not unheard of, and young writers should be on their guard against them. *Can* implies ability: *may* asks or gives permission.

Though this error belongs, as said, mostly to childhood's years, we find it occasionally in the work of the elders. Thus:

"Can I come in, Frank?" TROLLOPE, *Dr. Thorne*, Ch. xliv.

But here it is put into the mouth of a young speaker, and perhaps it should be said that this error does not rise much higher than the school-room. So high, however, it does rise, and somewhat too often.

21. Another error in the use of auxiliaries

Auxiliary without a verb. consists in leaving the auxiliary or helping word without anything to help.

" ' I 've sometimes thought she 'd turn me out of the house.'
" ' I wish with all my heart she had.' "

Hodgson, in his *Errors in the Use of English*, a large collection from English writers, has had better luck (or worse ?) in meeting with this blunder than I have had among American and English writers together. I am inclined to think it commoner in England than in America, and commoner fifty years ago than now. I cite a few of Hodgson's examples, with some of my own collecting:

"Shelley, like Byron, early knew what it was to love ; almost all the great poets have."

Have known, the writer meant to say, but there is no *known* in his sentence.

"We are all apt to imagine that what is, always has, and always will be."

Always has been is intended.

"I am anxious for the time when he will talk as much nonsense to me as I have to him."

"Some part of this exemption may, and no doubt is, due to mental and physical causes."

The analogy between this error and that which consists in leaving a pronoun without an antecedent is obvious, and the training that is good as a corrective for the one may be recommended for the other.

22. *Shall* and *will*. By far the most troublesome of the English auxiliaries are *shall* and

Shall and will. *will:* indeed, so common is the misuse of these two words that many persons question the wisdom of trying to maintain the distinction between them. As for me, however, I feel that the system of refined distinctions between these words which has grown up during five centuries and been perfected during the last two is a choice inheritance which everyone who cares for the beauties of his native tongue ought to be willing to make considerable effort to preserve.

That *will* originally implied desire and consequently determination, while *shall* expressed duty or obligation, is the key to the many nice shades of meaning that can now be expressed by the proper use of these two words. To trace out and explain all these nice distinctions would be an undertaking too large for these pages: only two or three of the plainest cases can be touched on.

a. Will can never be properly used in the first person, unless intention, purpose, or promise is implied. If nothing more is meant than that a given event is going to happen, *shall* must be used. This, the most simple and positive of the principles governing the use of *shall* and *will*, is violated in the recitation-room, daily, in the most flagrant way. Every hour I hear, " If we divide by the co-efficient of x we will find . . .", " Solving this equation we will find two values . . .", "If we look at Venus through a good telescope we will see it crescent-shaped," and so on.

Impossible as it is to listen to these things without shuddering, it is also impossible to pause to correct them all, and it ought not to be necessary: however difficult some of the other uses of these words may be, this distinction is of such an elementary kind as should be understood and correctly applied by everybody who pretends to be a student, and the neglect of it should be an unpardonable offence.

b. So positive and so simple is the principle just stated that it suffices to condemn at once and without appeal the use of *will* or *would* in the first person with such verbs as *like, prefer, wish, fear, hope,* and others expressing involuntary states of mind. " I would like to hear your opinion," " I would be afraid to walk there after dark," " I will expect to hear from you soon," " I would prefer to manage it in my own way," and all expressions like these are wrong. The state of feeling indicated, that of preferring, liking, fearing, is one that arises spontaneously in the speaker, and the will has no influence over it. That hundreds of such expressions can be found in the writings, and thousands in the speech, of men of considerable culture does not justify them: they are uniformly excluded from the writings of all who pay attention to correctness of style, from Shakspere to George Eliot. Such passages as the following, which may be found in any desired number in the reports of the transactions of scientific societies, have no justification, and no one who hopes to learn to speak and write English correctly should ever allow himself to use them:

"I would like to add a word to what Mr. Henderson has said."
"I would like to say just one word."
"Mr. Chairman, I would like the privilege of seconding that motion."

c. *Should* and *would*, when used affirmatively and in *direct* discourse (not in such expressions as "he said he should," "they thought they should"), follow the analogy of *shall* and *will*.

If these three principles be firmly grasped, most of the simpler uses of these words will present no difficulty.

Out of the original distinction between *shall* and *will*, the former expressing obligation and the latter determination, have arisen many subtle shades of distinction. It is in the expression of these refinements of meaning,—in interrogative forms, in indirect discourse, and in cases in which the words are used rather as independent verbs than as auxiliaries, that most of the real difficulties arise and that most of the supposed lapses of good writers occur. When better understood, however, these lapses are often found to be no lapses at all, but strictly in conformity with the correct use of the words. These refinements, interesting as the study of them is, it would be improper to try to present here. My present purpose will be accomplished if I can induce my readers to give to the simpler cases so much attention as will enable them to avoid the most conspicuous errors.

The following are examples, from daily papers, campaign speeches, and current literature, of the prevailing misuse of these words:

" Well, if the Legislature will agree to the amendments which I have suggested I will be glad to accept the charter."

" A few days ago, when he was asked why he did not openly fight Mr. Croker on questions of policy, he is reported to have replied that Mr. Croker had put him in the leadership and he would be an ingrate to turn against him."

" Ex-Secretary Whitney was asked if all the witnesses had been examined, and he said : ' No. We have not finished taking testimony, and I fear we will not to-day.' "

" If free coinage means a 100-cent dollar, equal to a gold dollar, . . . we will not then have cheap dollars, but dollars just like those we now have."

" We will be required to coin only that which is not needed elsewhere."

" We would look in vain through the speech delivered here one week ago to find a true statement of the issue . . ."

" If everything in the world be increased ten per cent. in value, why, we would pay ten per cent. in addition for what we would buy, and get ten per cent. more for what we would sell, and we would be in exactly the same place we occupied before."

" The election of 1892 was a great misfortune. It may be we would have had a collapse then, no one can be quite sure. But if we had we should never have gone so far or suffered so much."

Why the speaker should have repented him of *would* and returned to *should*, from which he ought not to have strayed, is not easy to understand, unless, following the example of some others, he is only trying to treat the rival auxiliaries impartially.

" Free silver would put more gold out of circulation than the mints of the United States could possibly bring in in years of silver, and instead of having more money we would have less. With our six hundred and odd millions of gold driven out of circulation, we will reduce the *per capita* money of this country between eight and nine dollars."

The speaker here uses both *would* and *will* wrongly; but he shows his willingness to be right sometimes, by saying, in another place:

" If Mr. Bryan . . . were in the Presidential

chair, without any legislation by Congress we should be on a silver basis in a week's time."

23. After these shocking utterances it will be a pleasure to note how the masters use these words:

> " ' We shall,
> As I conceive the journey, be at the Mount
> Before you, Lepidus.' "
> SHAKSPERE, *Ant. and Cleop.*, ii., 5.

" They know that we be hungry ; therefore are they gone out of the camp to hide themselves in the field, saying, when they come out of the city, we shall catch them alive, and get into the city." 2 Kings vii., 12.

" You need not offer me any inducements : I shall be delighted to come if I can." WILLIAM BLACK, *Briseis.*

" All Valentines are not foolish, and I shall not easily forget thine, my kind friend." CHARLES LAMB, " Valentine's Day."

" As soon as I get settled I will write and let you know, and I shall expect you immediately." DICKENS, *Pickwick Papers.*

" I was a coward on instinct. I shall think the better of myself and thee during my life." SHAK-SPERE, *Henry IV.*, I., ii., 4.

" I should only like to see what they 'd say to you if you were in a sponging-house ! Yes, I should

enjoy that, just to show that I 'm always right."
JERROLD, *Curtain Lectures*, No. 15.

"I know what men's two small glasses are. In a
little while you 'll have your face all over as if it
were made of red currant jam. And I should like
to know who is to endure you then?" *Ib.*, No. 3.

"What do you say? I made her blush at my
manners? I should like to have seen her blush."
Ib., No. 18.

". . . for which reason he shook him by the
hand, telling him he should be glad to see him at
his lodgings." ADDISON, *Spectator*.

" Well, it may be all very fine and philosophical,
but should n't I just like to read you the end of the
second volume of *Modern Painters*." RUSKIN,
The Ethics of the Dust, Lecture vii.

"' Well, Uncle,' said Tom, 'that is what I should
like to do.'" GEORGE ELIOT, *The Mill on the
Floss*, Ch. v.

"I wish I could have those minutes over again.
I wonder if I should really do what I think I should.
I should like to drive back and try it." BURNAND,
Happy Thoughts, Ch. xvii.

"I presented her with a book which I happened
to have with me, and I should not be pleased to
think that she forgot me." JOHNSON, *A Journey
to the Western Islands*.

"' I should like a turn with you, but it is a little
too late,' said he." HOPE, *The Prisoner of Zenda*.

"In America I should as soon think of drinking

pure alcohol directly after breakfast as a glass of porter." RICHARD GRANT WHITE, *England with-in and without.*

" ' You would n't like to sit to me for your portrait, should you ?' said Piero." GEORGE ELIOT, *Romola*, Ch. xxv.

"In regard to the waistcoat, I would n't have a man's waistcoat, much less a gentleman's waistcoat on my mind for no consideration ; but the silk handkerchief 's another thing ; and if you was satisfied when we get to Hounslow, I should n't object to that as a gift." DICKENS, *Martin Chuzzlewit*, Vol. II., Ch. xiii.

Dickens's lowest characters, if they are English, though they may be unable to manage other parts of their grammar, are always right in the use of *shall* and *will.*

"What ! Upon compulsion ?   No ; were I at the strappado, or all the racks in the world, I would not tell you on compulsion." SHAKSPERE, *Henry IV.*, I., ii., 4.

" ' I suppose I am dull about many things,' said Dorothea, simply.   'I should like to make life beautiful—I mean everybody's life.' " GEORGE ELIOT, *Middlemarch*, Ch. xxii.

" ' I hate grammar !   What 's the use of it ?'

" ' To teach you to speak and write correctly . . . Should you like to speak as old Job does ?' " *Ib.*, xxiv.

" ' I should not be surprised at anything in Bul-
strode, but I should be sorry to think it of Lyd-
gate.' " *Middlemarch*, Ch. xxvi.

" ' I should like to know when you left off,' said
Rosamund." *Ib.*, xxvii.

" I want to recall you to the subject of lotteries.
I should like to hear anybody maintain that they
are not very culpable transactions." HELPS, *Real-
mah*, Ch. vi.

24. Since Shakspere's day the use of the
possessive form where no possession is to be
expressed has been greatly extended.
Possessive.
For a long while " its " was stoutly
resisted as a needless innovation; now, not only
is this word thoroughly established, but our
ready-writers put almost any word into the
possessive form, without regard to possession
or to euphony either, and the preposition " of "
seems to be falling into disuse. We read
now—" Negotiations are pending between the
powers' representatives and the Porte," " The
Charter Commission's end," " The test of the
suggestion's efficiency might be made there,"
" Sorosis' president," " The State of Georgia's

loss," "The Administration's view of the commission's make-up," and much more of the same kind.

How unnecessary these harsh utterances are, becomes plain when we note how easy it is to avoid them.

" Negotiations are pending between the Porte and the representatives of the powers," " The end of the Charter Commission," " The efficiency (value) of the suggestion," " The loss of the State of Georgia." Surely all these express the thought intended, and all more euphoniously than the expressions cited.

The following it is hardly worth while to correct :

"Rapid transit by the Elm Street underground railroad is, we believe, assured by yesterday's confirmation by the Appellate Division of the Supreme Court commission's report in approval of the Rapid Transit Commission's plans. Despite the rejoicings of the Manhattan Elevated Railway Company's officials, we believe that the remarkable qualifications of the Division's judgment present no obstacle to the project which time, patience, and the extraordinary powers of the Rapid Transit Commission may not surmount.

"Yet we believe that the Appellate Division's additions to the law's restrictions will not be found of paralyzing effect."

25. It will perhaps be thought by some that such faults as I have illustrated are too trifling to deserve attention. It is, of course, true that they can be avoided only by waiting and picking and choosing, and it is true that, sometimes, there is not time for such care. This is the apology for the writers of the newspaper press and all who are compelled to write in haste; and, though not a justification, it is sometimes a fair excuse. It is indeed an occasion for wonder, when one thinks how a daily paper is prepared, that it is so well written as it generally is. But after all, haste does not excuse everything, and proper training, the acquired habit of looking out constantly for false references and false agreements, for well-known improprieties, for vulgarisms and useless innovations, the habit of holding in the

youthful pen (and the elderly pen too for that matter) rather than give it free course, will enable the writer to avoid easily many an awkward turn which he at first deems inevitable or at least excusable. It is to assist in the formation of this habit that this little work is intended.

At the suggestion of my publishers, I append the following Index, which contains, in addition to the expressions criticised in the preceding chapters, others that in my opinion should also be condemned. I strongly recommend to every writer, and particularly to every young writer, to keep such an Index on hand, and to interest himself in making to it needful additions.

INDEX EXPURGATORIUS.

Above, for more than.
Antagonize, for oppose.
Any, for at all : " She does not walk any if she can
    avoid it." " I don't work any at night."
Apt, for liable or likely.

Balance, for rest or remainder.
Be done with, for have done with.
Bogus, for worthless, fraudulent.
But, for only : " others but nodded."

Cablegram, for cable despatch or message.
Calculated to, for likely to or fit to.
Carnival, as metaphor.
Claim, for assert or maintain.
Cyclone, for tornado or hurricane.

Deputize, for depute.
Develops, for turns out : " It develops that Senator
    Hoar introduced the proposed amendment."
Due to, for owing to.

Electrocute, for kill by electricity.
Endorse, for approve.
En route, for on the way.
Enthuse over, for feel enthusiastic over, or admire.

Every now and then, for now and then.
Every once in a while, for once in a while.
Expect, for think or suppose, relating to present
time.

Fix, for adjust, repair, and a hundred other words.
Folks, for folk or people : " the good folks at the
inn," for "the good people at the inn."
Fraud, for impostor..

Goes without saying, for is understood.
Gratuitous, for unnecessary.

Have got, for have.
Hire, let, lease. (See dictionaries.)

Inaugurate, for begin or open.
In evidence, for conspicuous.
In our midst, for in the midst of us, or among us.
Inside of, for within or in less than : "inside of
two weeks."

Jeopardize, for endanger.

Know as, for know that : " I do not know as I can
say much on that subject."

Learn, for teach.
Leave, for let.
Lengthy, for long.
Loan, for lend.
Locate, for settle or place.
Lurid, for bright or brilliant.

Majority, for most : " The majority of the stock is
   worthless."
Materialize, for appear.
Murderous, for deadly : "murderous weapons."
Mutual, for common.

Observe, for say (it means to heed or attend to).
Official, for officer.

Patron, for customer.
Posted, for informed.
Proven, for proved.

Quite, for very.

Reliable, for trustworthy.
Remains, for corpse.
Rendition, for performance.
Repudiate, for reject or disown.
Restive, for restless or frisky.
Resurrect, for bring back to life.
Retire, for go to bed.
Retire, for withdraw (active verb).
Rôle, for part.
Ruination, for ruin or destruction.

Since, for ago : " It happened more than a year
   since."
Some, for somewhat or a little : "It thawed some."
State, for say : " He stated that he had no property
   of his own."
Stop at, for stay at.

Those kind, for that kind.
Transference, for transfer.
Transpire, for occur or take place.

Ventilate, for expose or explain.

Will be able, for shall be able, in the first person.
Would like, for should like, in the first person.

INDEX

LANGUAGE

THE ENGLISH LANGUAGE AND ENGLISH GRAMMAR.

An Historical Study of the Sources, Development, and Analogies of the Language, and of the Principles Covering its Usages. Illustrated by Copious Examples by Writers of all Periods. By SAMUEL RAMSEY. 8° $2.00

"Mr. Ramsey's work will appeal especially to those that desire to know something more about the history and philology, the growth and mistakes of their native tongue than is given in the ordinary text-books."—*Baltimore Sun.*

"To have completed such a work is almost reward enough for the pains expended upon it. The book will be regarded as an authority on the history of the English language and English grammar."—*N. Y. Observer.*

SOME COMMON ERRORS OF SPEECH.

By ALFRED G. COMPTON, Professor in College of the City of New York. 12° . . . . $

Suggestions for the avoiding of certain classes of errors, with examples of bad and of good usage.

A SIMPLE GRAMMAR OF ENGLISH NOW IN USE.

By JOHN EARLE, A.M., LL.D., Professor of Anglo-Saxon, University of Oxford, author of "English Prose : Its Elements, History, and Usage." 12° $1.50

ORTHOMETRY.

A Treatise on the Art of Versification and the Technicalities of Poetry, with a New and Complete Rhyming Dictionary. By R. F. BREWER, B.A. 12°, pp. xv. + 376 . . . . . . $2.00

"It is a good book for its purpose, lucid, compact, and well arranged. It lays bare, we believe, the complete anatomy of poetry. It affords interesting quotations, in the way of example, and interesting comments by distinguished critics upon certain passages from the distinguished poets."—*N. Y. Sun.*

MANUAL OF LINGUISTICS.

An Account of General and English Phonology. By JOHN CLARK, A.M. 8°, pp. lxiii. + 314 . . . . $2.00

"Mr. Clark has traced the English language back to its foundations in his work 'Manual of Linguistics.' It is an interesting theme, and his book will prove very useful for reference, for he has culled from many sources and gone over a wide territory."—*Detroit Free Press.*

COMPOSITION IN THE SCHOOL-ROOM.

A Practical Treatise. By E. GALBRAITH. 16°, cloth . . $1.00

"The author has drawn fully from the best writers on the subject, and her book is an epitome of the best thought of all."—*Boston Transcript.*

G. P. PUTNAM'S SONS, NEW YORK AND LONDON.

WORKS BY W. H. PHYFE

HOW SHOULD I PRONOUNCE ?

Or the Art of Correct Pronunciation. 16° $1.25

    Popular edition, 16° . . . . 75 cts.

"I appreciate its value, and indorse your work as a most serviceable aid to all who wish to speak our language correctly."—EDWIN BOOTH.

THE SCHOOL PRONOUNCER.

Based on Webster's Unabridged Dictionary. 16°, pp. 366 . $1.25

"A scholarly and scientific presentation of a most difficult subject."—Prof. T. W. HUNT, College of New Jersey.

SEVEN THOUSAND WORDS OFTEN MISPRONOUNCED.

A guide to correct pronunciation. Fourth revised edition (43rd thousand), with supplement of 1400 additional words. 16° . . $1.00

"A complete and conveniently arranged hand-book of the difficulties in English pronunciation."—*Cambridge Tribune.*

"It is compiled with great industry and a careful study of authorities, as well as an enlightened application to special and first-handed sources of information, and I am confident that it will contribute, as you intend, toward a more accurate pronunciation of our language."—Prof. W. D. WHITNEY, Yale College, editor of the *Century Dictionary.*

THE TEST PRONOUNCER.

A companion volume to "7000 Words Often Mispronounced," containing the identical list of words found in the larger work, arranged in groups of ten, without diacritical marks for convenience in recitations. 16° . . . . 50 cts.

"This last volume was prepared at the suggestion of many teachers, and it will be found of great value to others as well. It is admirable in purpose, and supplements completely the previous work."—*Boston Times.*

5000 WORDS COMMONLY MISSPELLED.

A carefully selected list of words difficult to spell, together with directions for spelling, and for the division of words into syllables; with an appendix containing the rules and list of amended spellings recommended by the Philological Society of London, and the American Philological Association. 16° . . . . 75 cts.

"This book is a work of reference, and will be found very useful. It contains a carefully selected list of words difficult to spell. . . . The simple rules given, with suggestions, are admirable."—*Minneapolis Tribune.*

"This list of words often misspelled has been selected with the utmost care."—*Detroit Free Press.*

G. P. PUTNAM'S SONS, NEW YORK AND LONDON,